cloverleaf books™

Stories with Character

In Your Shoes
A Story of Empathy

Kristin Johnson

illustrated by Mike Byrne

M MILLBROOK PRESS • MINNEAPOLIS

To my friend and fellow writer
Sandi Clough —K.J.

To Oscar & Harry —M.B.

Millbrook Press
A division of Lerner Publishing Group, Inc.
241 First Avenue North
Minneapolis, MN 55401 USA

For reading levels and more information, look up this title at
www.lernerbooks.com.

Main body text set in Slappy Inline 22/28.
Typeface provided by T26.

Library of Congress Cataloging-in-Publication Data

Names: Johnson, Kristin F., 1968- author. | Byrne, Mike, 1979–
    illustrator.
Title: In your shoes : a story of empathy / by Kristin Johnson ;
    illustrated by Mike Byrne.
Description: Minneapolis : Millbrook Press, [2018] | Series:
    Cloverleaf books - stories with character | Audience: Age 5–8.
    | Audience: K to grade 3. | Includes bibliographical references
    and index.
Identifiers: LCCN 2017009219 (print) | LCCN 2017036123
    (ebook) | ISBN 9781512498226 (eb pdf) | ISBN
    9781512486476 (lb : alk. paper)
Subjects: LCSH: Empathy—Juvenile literature.
Classification: LCC BF575.E55 (ebook) | LCC BF575.E55 J64
    2018 (print) | DDC 152.4/1—dc23

LC record available at https://lccn.loc.gov/2017009219

Manufactured in the United States of America
1-43471-33211-8/14/2017

TABLE OF CONTENTS

Chapter One

My Exciting News

I'm so excited!

My family just got a pet rabbit!

When I get to school, I rush over to my friend Jacob to tell him.

"That's really cool, Sophie!" he says. "I have some news too. And it's important."

"But first let me tell you about my rabbit!" I say.

"Sophie, wait—" Jacob starts. But I have so much to say that I keep on talking.

"Never mind!" Jacob storms away.

It is important to listen to others' thoughts and feelings.

Chapter Two

Show-and-Tell

In my class, the day always starts with show-and-tell. Our teacher, Ms. Rhee, says sharing is a good way to start a morning.

Jacob shares first. But I can't stop thinking about my rabbit.

I don't hear what Jacob says.
I decide I can ask him later.

Finally, it's my turn to share! I tell the class all about my new rabbit.

I tell what my rabbit eats and how we take care of him. I tell everyone how my family is picking out a name.

Everyone seems excited. But Jacob stays quiet.

Why isn't my friend excited for me?

When I sit down again, our friend Emma puts a hand on Jacob's shoulder. "I'll miss you," she says.

What could Emma mean?

Chapter Three

What I Missed

"What did I miss?" I ask Emma and Jacob later that day at recess.

"Sophie, I'm moving," Jacob says.

"What?" I say. "Why didn't you tell me?"
"I tried," he says. "You wouldn't listen."

Empathy means understanding another person's feelings.

I missed Jacob's announcement,
and now I'm really going to miss him.

I should have been more thoughtful.

How would I feel in his shoes?

Thinking about how you would feel in someone else's shoes is an example of having empathy.

Chapter Four
Making It Right

The next day, I apologize to Jacob for not thinking about his feelings. I promise to write to him when he moves away.

"That would be great!" Jacob says.

"You can come over to play before you go," I tell him. "And you can tell me about your new home! This time, I'll listen to **every word**."

"That sounds fun," Jacob says.
"Can I see your new rabbit too?"
"Of course!"

Jacob smiles. "Thanks for thinking about me, Sophie," he says. "You're a really good friend."

Put It in Writing!

Just like Sophie and Jacob are going to write to each other, you can write to express your feelings.

Write a letter to someone you would like to get to know or to someone you want to reconnect with. Use a sheet of paper and a pencil, or type it on a computer.

GLOSSARY

announcement: news someone shares

apologize: to say you are sorry about something

empathy: understanding or caring about what someone else is feeling or experiencing

sharing: to tell or explain something to others to express yourself

thoughtful: kind and considering other people's feelings and needs

BOOKS

de la Peña, Matt. *Last Stop on Market Street.* New York: G. P. Putnam's Sons, 2015. Ride the bus through town with CJ and his grandma in this story. Together, they try to see their community through other people's eyes.

Nelson, Robin. *How Can I Help? A Book about Caring*. Minneapolis: Lerner Publications, 2014. Find out ways you can put yourself in someone else's shoes and some things you can do to show you care.

Sornson, Bob. *Stand in My Shoes: Kids Learning about Empathy*. Golden, CA: Love and Logic, 2013. Read this story to find out how Emily learns what empathy means and why it matters.

WEBSITES

Feelings
http://kidshealth.org/en/kids/feeling
Get answers to questions you have about your feelings and how to handle them.

Kid Videos
https://www.stopbullying.gov/kids/webisodes/index.html
Put yourself in someone else's place by watching videos about bullying situations. Free online quizzes let you apply what you learned.